W9-CMZ-437

"THE ADVENTURES OF THUMBS UP JOHNNIE!®"

JOHNNIE FINDS A BUDDY ©

www.thumbsupjohnnie.com

This book is dedicated to my parents, Kay & Kerry Walbridge, who have whole-heartedly accepted and encouraged my creative spirit. Their support has allowed me to " keep the dream alive!"

To my husband, Wayne Klenke who endures my constant "dream state" and supports me residing there.

To Alex Hart, Chris Kostman, Sharon & Kim Tucci, who believed in this project before it ever sold book one.

Michelle Bain

Thumbs Up Johnnie is a happy little thumbprint with a good life and comfortable cowboy boots! He is a sweet fellow who loves working at his restaurant, The Long Horn Diner, where he greets hungry folks and flips the "biggest flapjacks in Texas."

Johnnie loves his life in Happy, Texas, where he visits all of his friends on Lone Star Row. They shop and greet one another with friendly tips of their hats and a "Howdy, hello!"

Johnnie spent all morning flipping flapjacks. Afterwards, he decided to visit one of his favorite stores on Lone Star Row, a place called Dime Store Sam's.

Johnnie loved Dime Store Sam's because Sam had all the fun stuff! The last time he was there, Johnnie bought a new kite, a glow-in-the-dark yo-yo, and his prized possession: a lucky lasso.

4

"*H*ello, Dime Store Sam! How's the day treating you?" asked Johnnie.

"Fine and dandy!" said Dime Store Sam, beaming a hundred-dollar smile. "The sun's a-shinin,' and I got a new shipment of sweet treats. How about a taste?"

"I'm always up for a sweet treat. Thank you so much!" said Johnnie. He eagerly accepted the bag of goodies, gave Sam a "thumbs up," and waved goodbye.

5

Johnnie skipped down Lone Star Row to see Banker Bill at the Lucky Horseshoe Bank. Everyday, Johnnie saved some money from the diner and put it in his savings account.

"Good afternoon, Banker Bill! I'd like to make a deposit," said Johnnie, handing Bill the bag of money.

"That's wonderful! A dollar saved is a dollar earned, Johnnie," assured Bill.

"By the way, those special silver dollar flapjacks were delicious this morning. A good breakfast sure helps me concentrate when I'm countin' money here at the bank!" said Bill.

8

"Well, I'm glad you liked 'em, Bill!" said Johnnie.

After Banker Bill deposited the money, he proudly announced, "The Lucky Horseshoe Bank is fifty years old today! To celebrate, we're giving each of our loyal customers a set of four lucky horseshoes."

Johnnie was so surprised! He felt a tickle in his stomach as he thought to himself, "What am I going to do with such a wonderful gift?"

"Thank you Banker Bill!" exclaimed Johnnie as he waved goodbye and gave him a "thumbs up."

Thumbs Up Johnnie's next stop was the Rumblin' Tummy Bakery. Cookies are Johnnie's favorite treat, and the Rumblin' Tummy Bakery has the best in Texas. Johnnie is best friends with the owner, Lillian Pinky. Johnnie calls her "L'il Pinky" for short.

"Howdy L'il Pinky!" said Johnnie as he walked through the bakery door. "It smells yummy in here! What's baking today?"

"Well Johnnie, I am baking apple pie, sugar cookies, and angel food cake today!" said L'il Pinky. "Would you like a cookie?"

"Yes I would!" Thumbs Up Johnnie giggled. "I've had a great day today, L'il. I got some free candy from Dime Store Sam, lucky horseshoes from Banker Bill, and now a yummy treat from you!"

L'il Pinky smiled at Thumbs Up Johnnie and said, "Sounds like it is your lucky day! What do you plan to do with your horseshoes?"

"Well, I reckon I could hang them above my doorway for good luck!" replied Johnnie.

"I have an idea," offered L'il Pinky. "Your boots are gettin' worn from walkin' back and forth to the diner every day. How about gettin' a horse? Then you could save your energy for cooking flapjacks."

15

$\mathcal{J}$ohnnie realized why he liked L'il Pinky so much . . .

because she was always thinking! He wondered to himself,

"My boots are gettin' worn . . . I've always wanted a horse . . .

I have four brand new horseshoes . . . why not?"

"That's a great idea! Where would I get one?" asked Johnnie.

L'il Pinky grinned with delight. "My uncle has a horse ranch over in Spur, Texas. I reckon you could find a horse there, Johnnie."

He was so excited about going to a horse ranch. Johnnie shouted, "Can we go tomorrow?"

L'il Pinky arranged with her uncle to visit the ranch the next day and pick out a horse for Johnnie.

"Tomorrow I'll have a horse of my very own!" thought Johnnie.

Thumbs Up Johnnie was so excited he could hardly sleep that night! It was just like the day he bought his first cowboy hat and boots. He slept with one eye open, waiting for the sun to come up.

22

The next morning, Johnnie couldn't wait to hear L'il Pinky knock on his front door. He ran to the door, almost slipping out of his boots. "Hello, L'il! I'm ready for our trip to Tumbleweed Ranch!"

"Yes, I'm ready too. I packed some goodies from the bakery and grabbed some carrots for the horses. Let's go find you a horse, Johnnie!"

*A*nd so they were off to Tumbleweed Ranch to find

Thumbs Up Johnnie his new horse…

26

"*W*ow! Tumbleweed Ranch is beautiful," Johnnie said. "I'm sure I'll find a horse here."

"Oh, yes, I think so," said L'il Pinky. "My uncle loves horses and takes tender, loving care of each one!"

Thumbs Up Johnnie was so excited he was shaking in his boots. He couldn't wait to get to the barn!

"*H*owdy!" hollered a voice from the barn. L'il Pinky knew it was Uncle Bob. His friends called him Bronco Bob.

He had worked with horses all his life. He knew each horse had its own personality, a "special something" that made it unique.

"I have a lot of good horses in the barn, Johnnie," said Bronco Bob. "Let's take a look inside. I'm sure we'll find you one."

Thumbs Up Johnnie and L'il Pinky walked through the barn and fed carrots to the horses. They were strong and healthy horses who looked happy and content.

*B*ut in one stall they noticed a little horse standing in the corner with a sad expression.

"What about this little guy, Uncle Bob? He looks so sad," said L'il Pinky.

"Poor little fella. He's lonely," Bronco Bob replied. "His sister left two weeks ago to live with a young girl. His best friend went to live at the farm next door. Now they only get to see each other every once in while."

*B*ronco Bob opened up the stall and said in a gentle voice, "Hey, boy…cheer up! My niece and her friend would like to give you a treat. Come on, boy, turn around and say howdy to them."

The horse turned around and looked up at Thumbs Up Johnnie and L'il Pinky. He blinked slowly with his big, brown eyes, as if to say "hello."

Thumbs Up Johnnie asked Bronco Bob, "What's this little fella's name?"

*B*ronco Bob replied, "His name is Buddy." Bronco Bob took the bridle and led the horse to L'il Pinky and Johnnie. L'il Pinky walked towards Buddy and put a carrot underneath his nose. Buddy looked at her with his big, brown eyes and blinked very slowly as if to say, "Thank you, Ma'am."

Buddy just knew by looking at L'il Pinky that she was nice. He also smelled her freshly baked muffins in the picnic basket and hoped she would feed him one of those!

Thumbs Up Johnnie walked up to Buddy and put his hand under the horse's nose. Buddy twitched his nose and made a loud "neigh," which sounded like "hello." Johnnie began gently scratching Buddy's nose and tickling his whiskers. The two were instant pals.

Bronco Bob could tell that Buddy was happy. "Do you like the little fella?" he asked.

Thumbs Up Johnnie replied, "Sure do! I know just the kind of nose scratching he loves. Bronco Bob, I would really like to take Buddy home with me to my ranch."

"Sure," Bronco Bob replied. "I would love for you to take him home, but you have to pledge to always take care of Buddy."

41

They had found the perfect horse! L'il Pinky and Thumbs Up Johnnie packed up their basket and put a blanket and saddle on Buddy. Johnnie hopped up onto Buddy and gave a "thumbs up" to Bronco Bob.

"Goodbye," said Bronco Bob.

Thumbs Up Johnnie was glad he could give his new "Buddy" a home. "Hmmm, I hope he likes my flapjacks," thought Johnnie.

*I*t had been one of the best days of Johnnie's life! He had spent the entire day with his best friend, L'il Pinky, and he felt certain his new pal, Buddy, would be the perfect horse for him.

As the three of them walked back home through Bluebonnet Pasture, Johnnie was so excited that he felt butterflies in his tummy. He was sure that many fun adventures with his friends were just about to begin.

46